ART OF COLOURING

ROGUE ONE
A *STAR WARS* STORY

100 IMAGES TO INSPIRE CREATIVITY

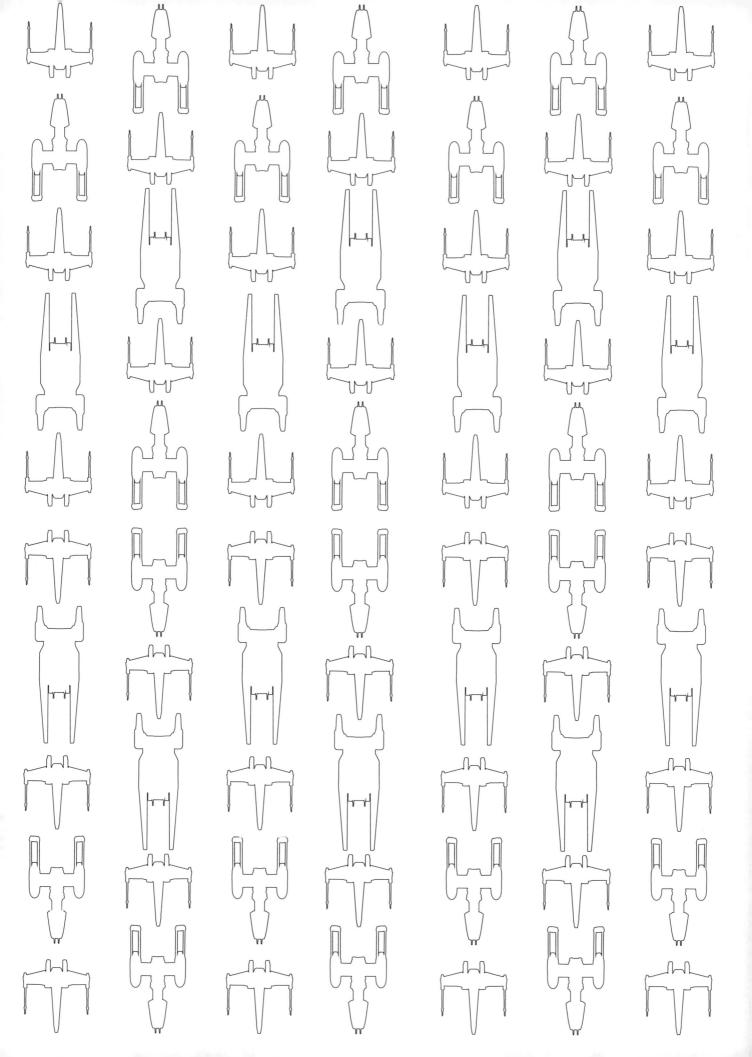

JYN ERSO

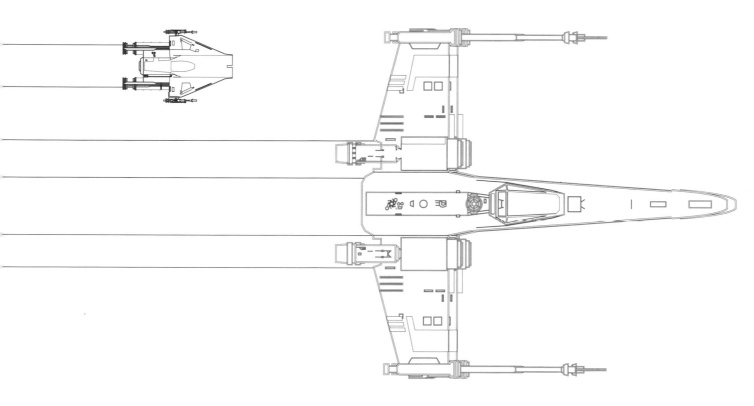
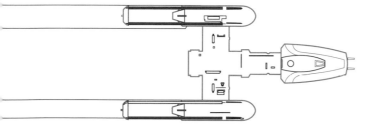

CASSIAN ANDOR

K-2SO

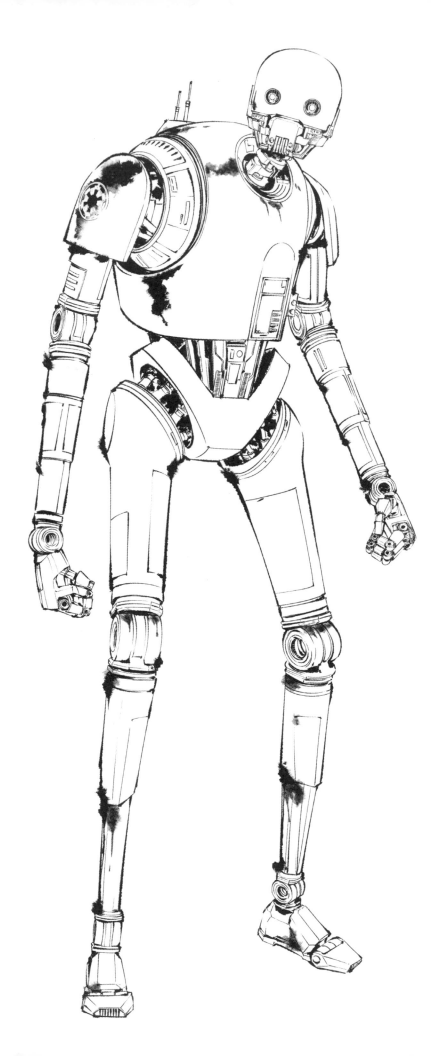

BAZE MALBUS

CHIRRUT ÎMWE

DEATH

TROOPER

IMPERIAL
DIRECTOR

DEFENCE
KRENNIC

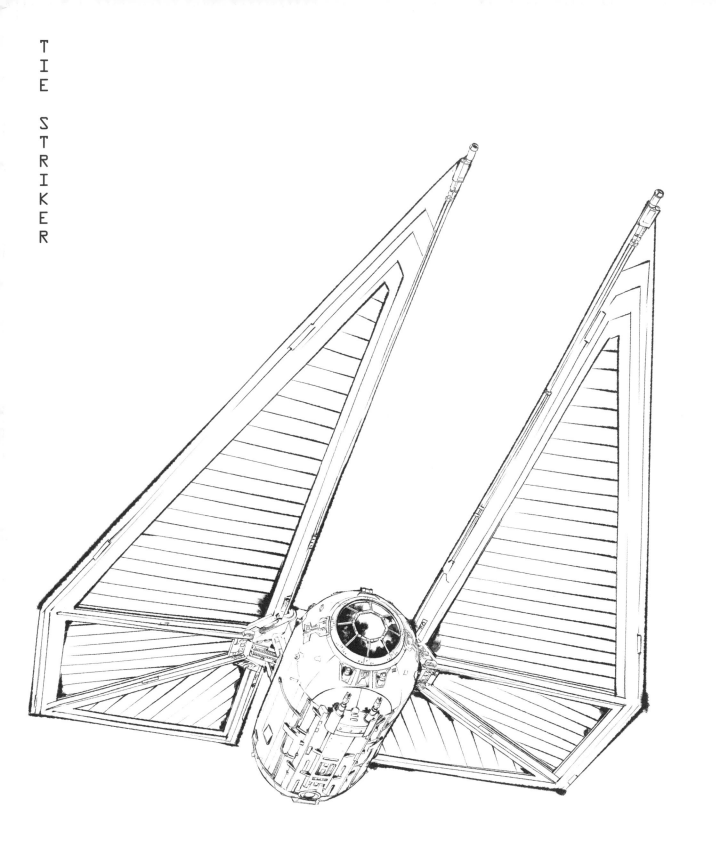

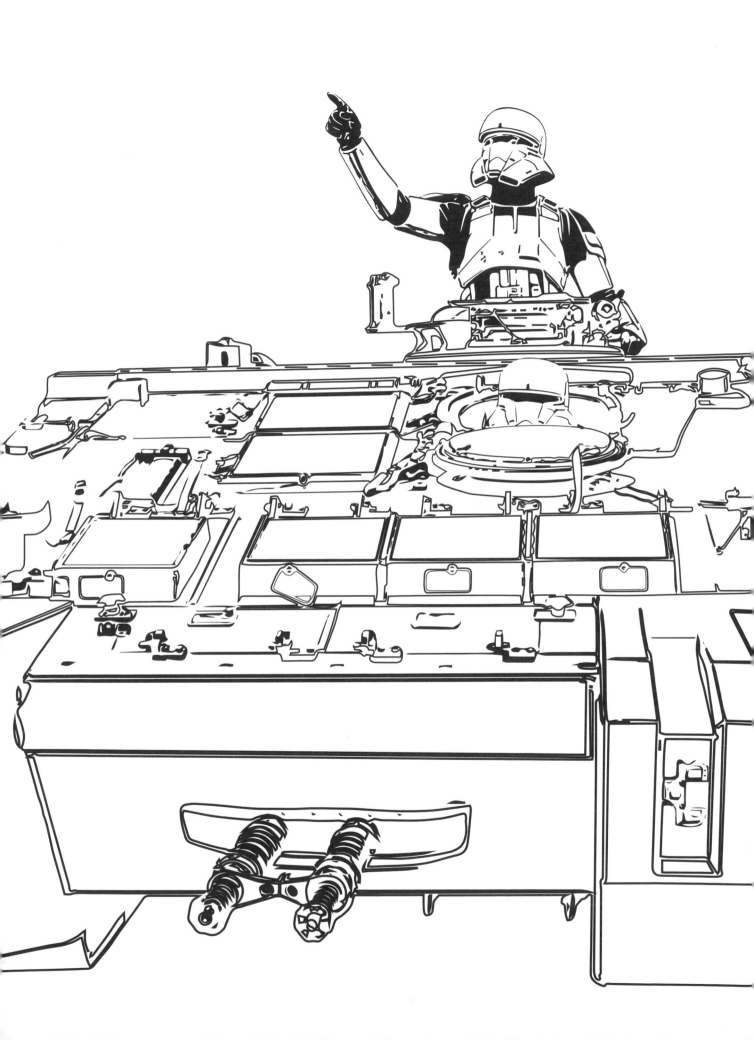

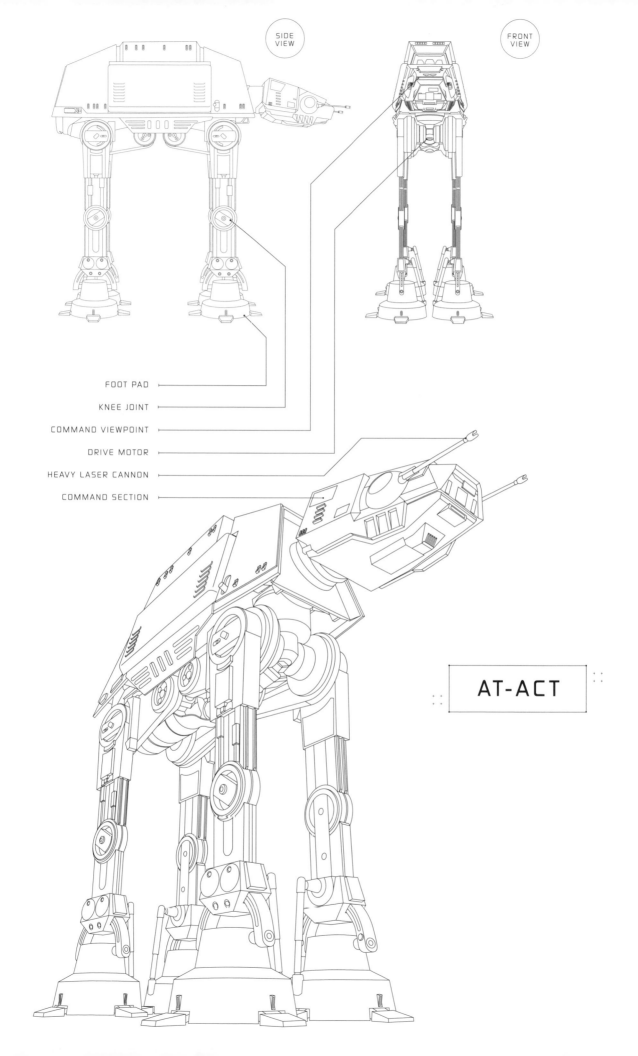

SIDE
VIEW

FRONT
VIEW

FOOT PAD
KNEE JOINT
COMMAND VIEWPOINT
DRIVE MOTOR
HEAVY LASER CANNON
COMMAND SECTION

AT-ACT

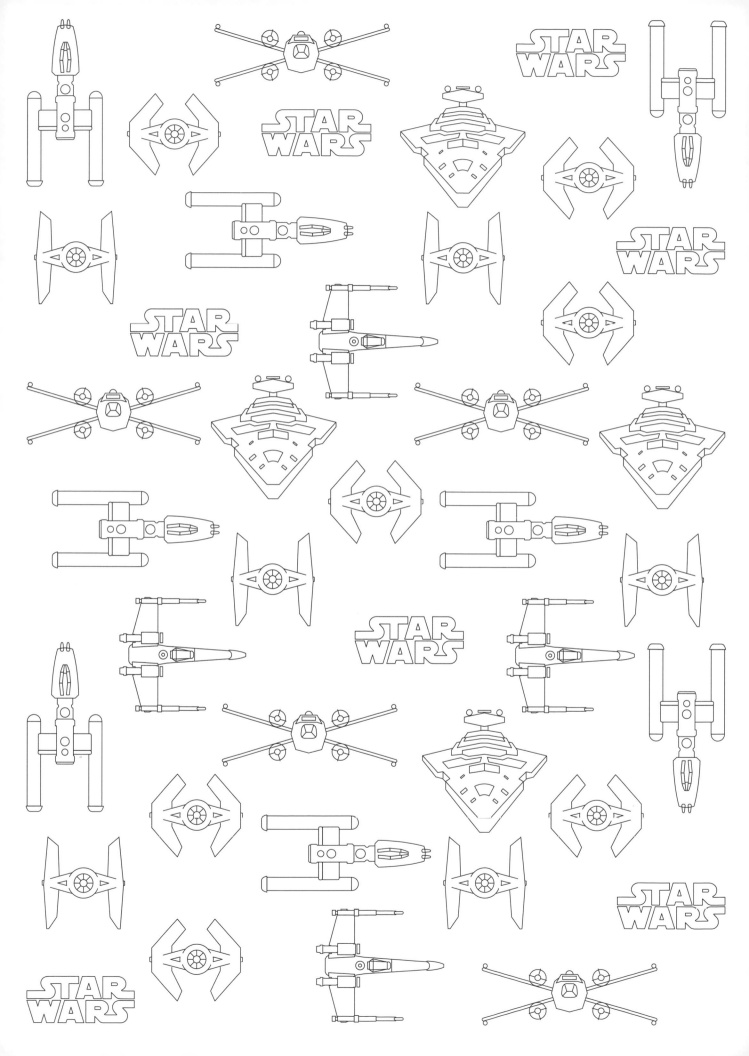

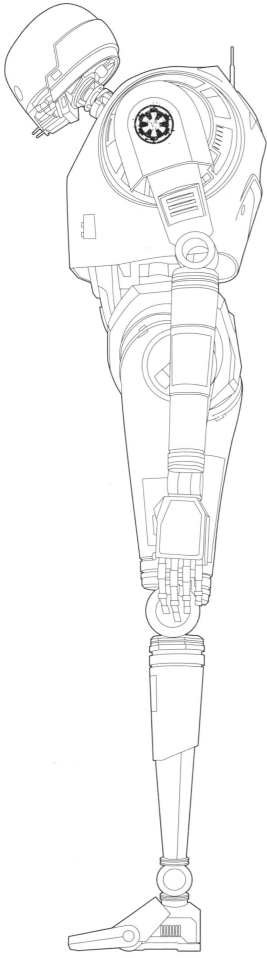
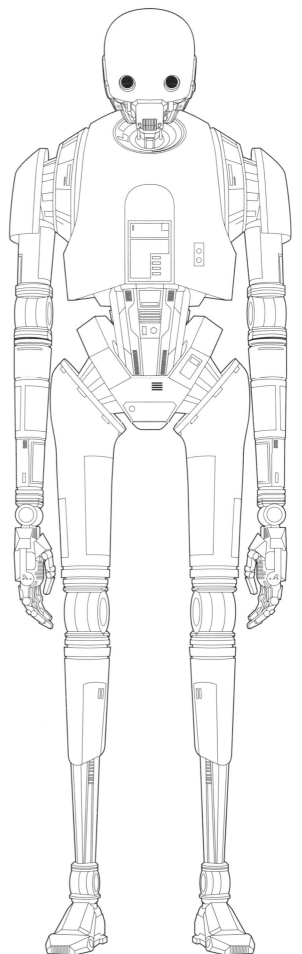

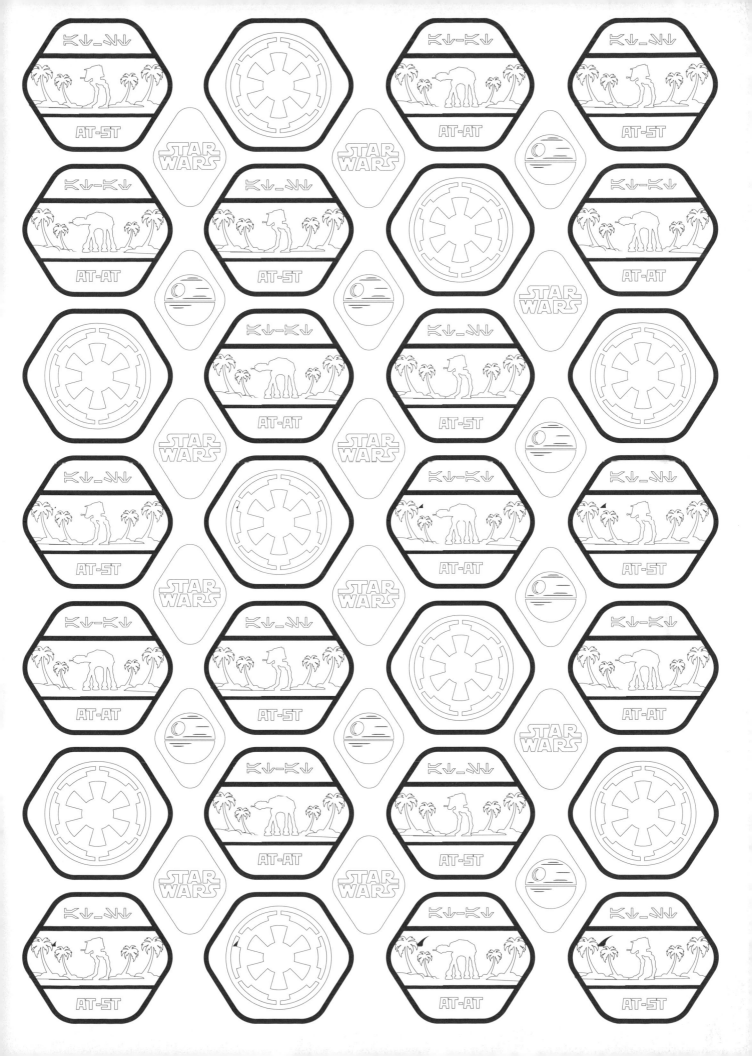

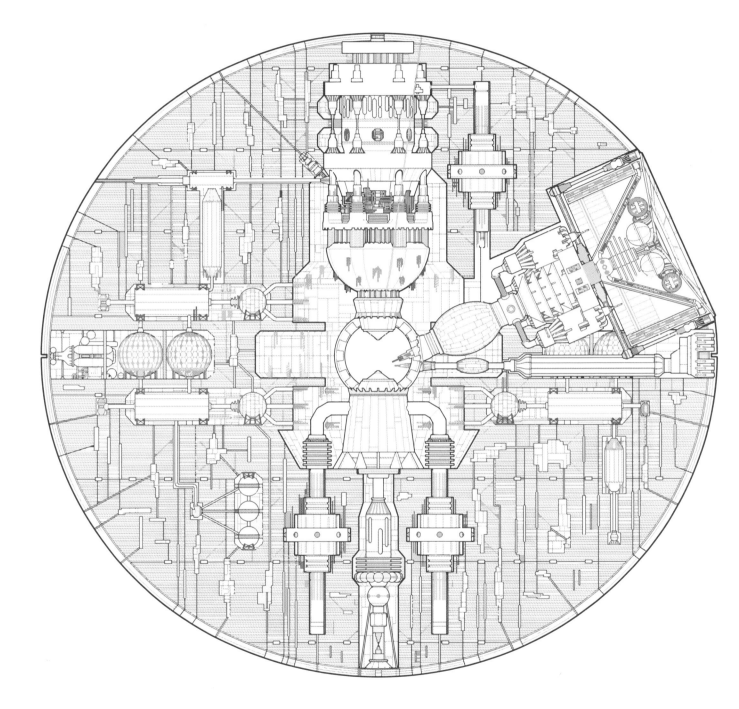

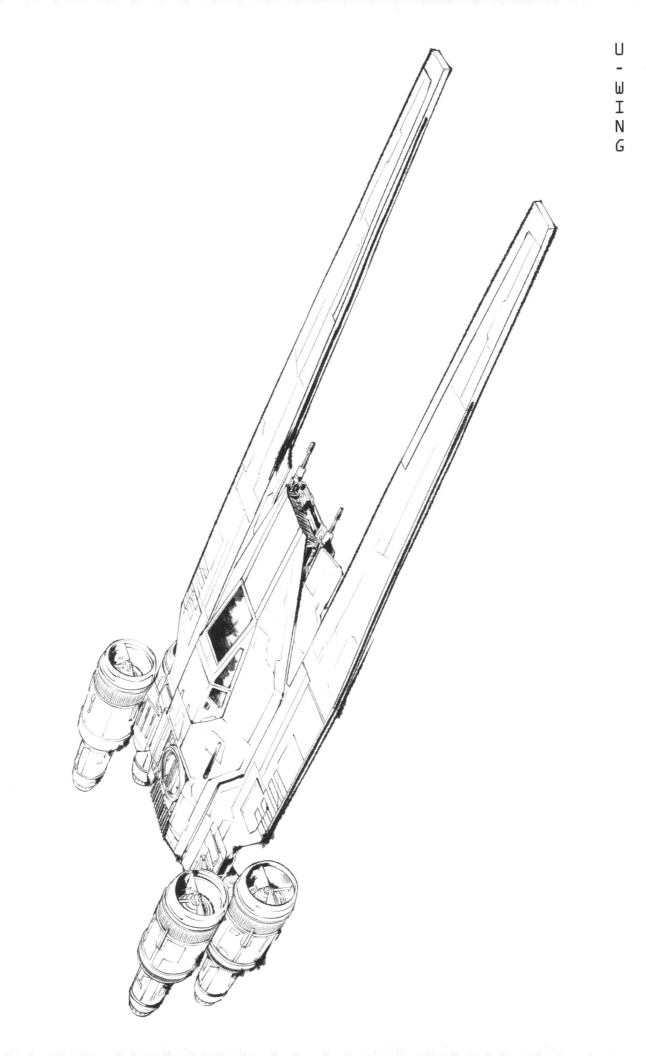

GALEN ERSO

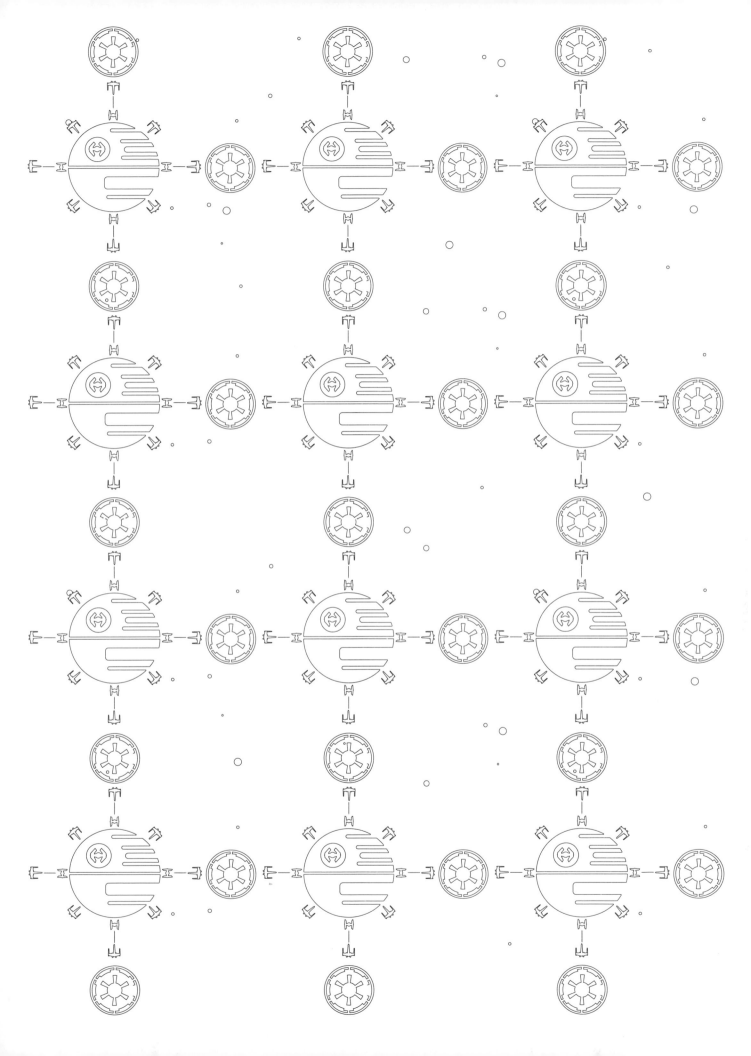

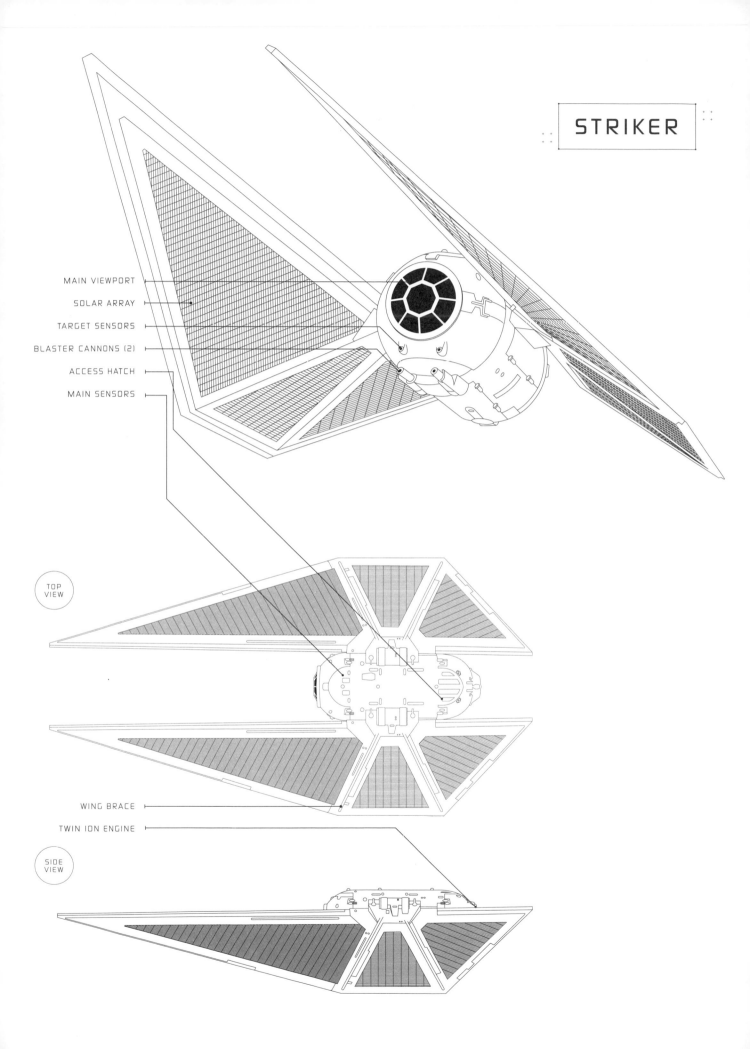

STRIKER

MAIN VIEWPORT

SOLAR ARRAY

TARGET SENSORS

BLASTER CANNONS (2)

ACCESS HATCH

MAIN SENSORS

TOP
VIEW

WING BRACE

TWIN ION ENGINE

SIDE
VIEW

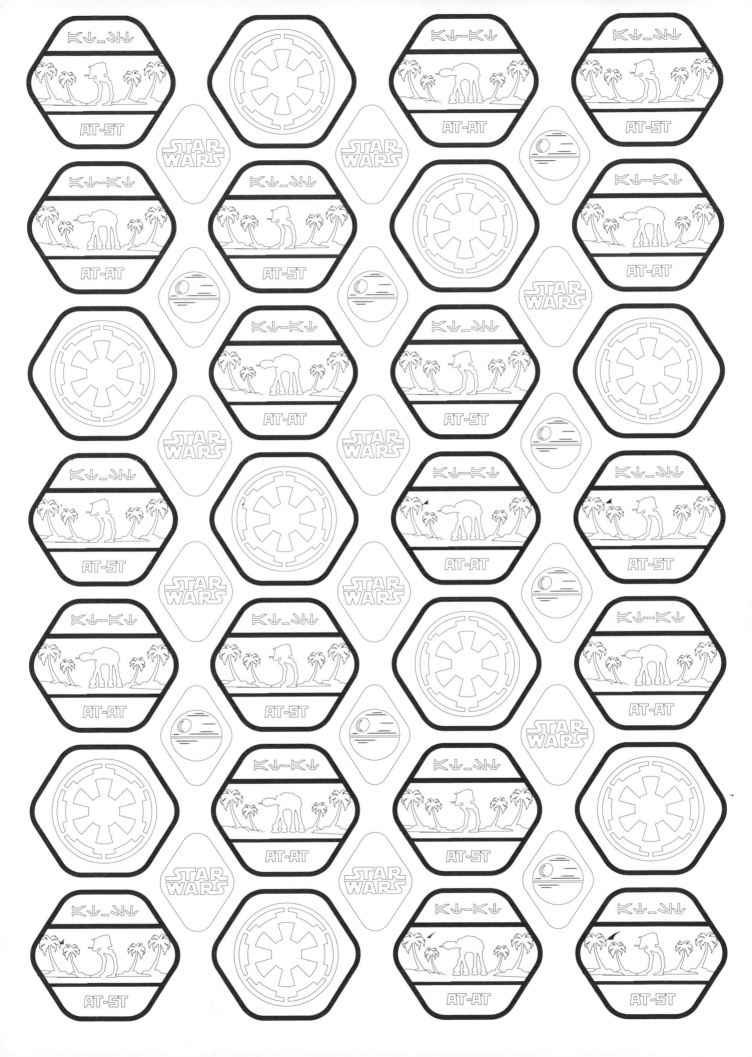

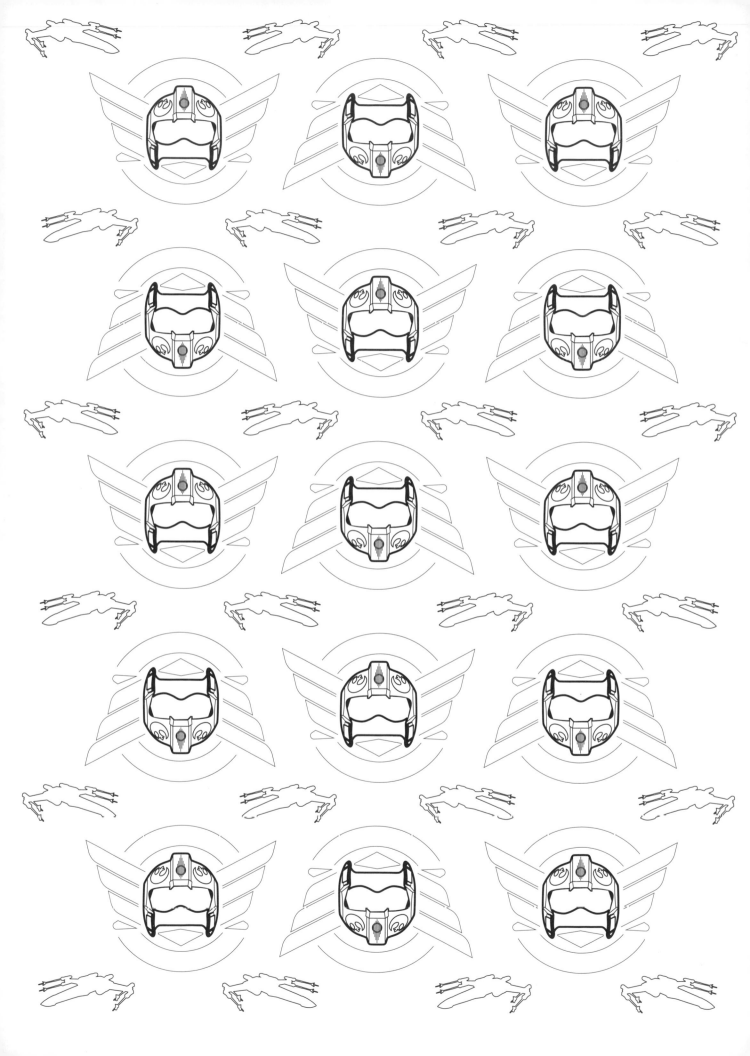

EDRIO TWO TUBES

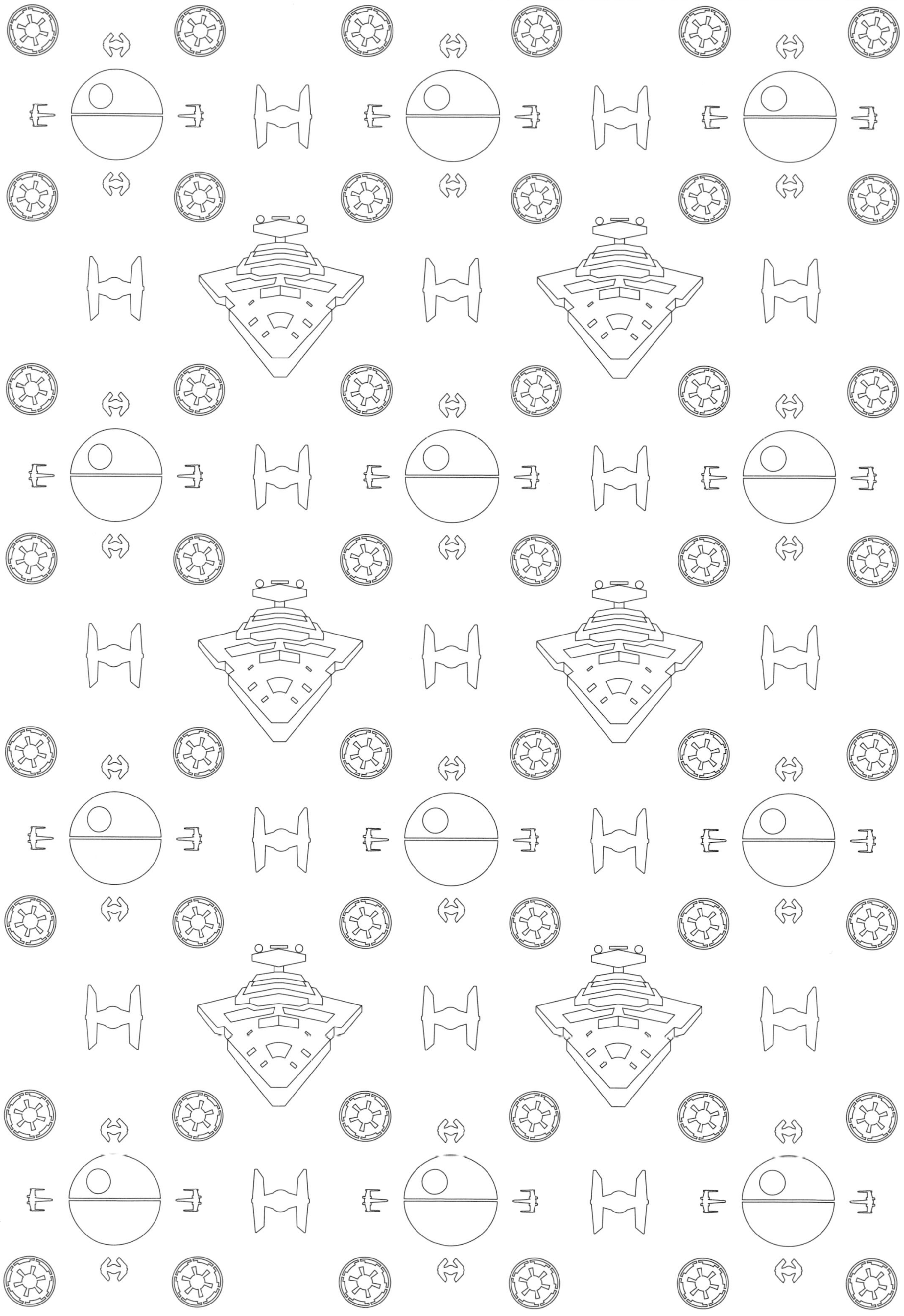

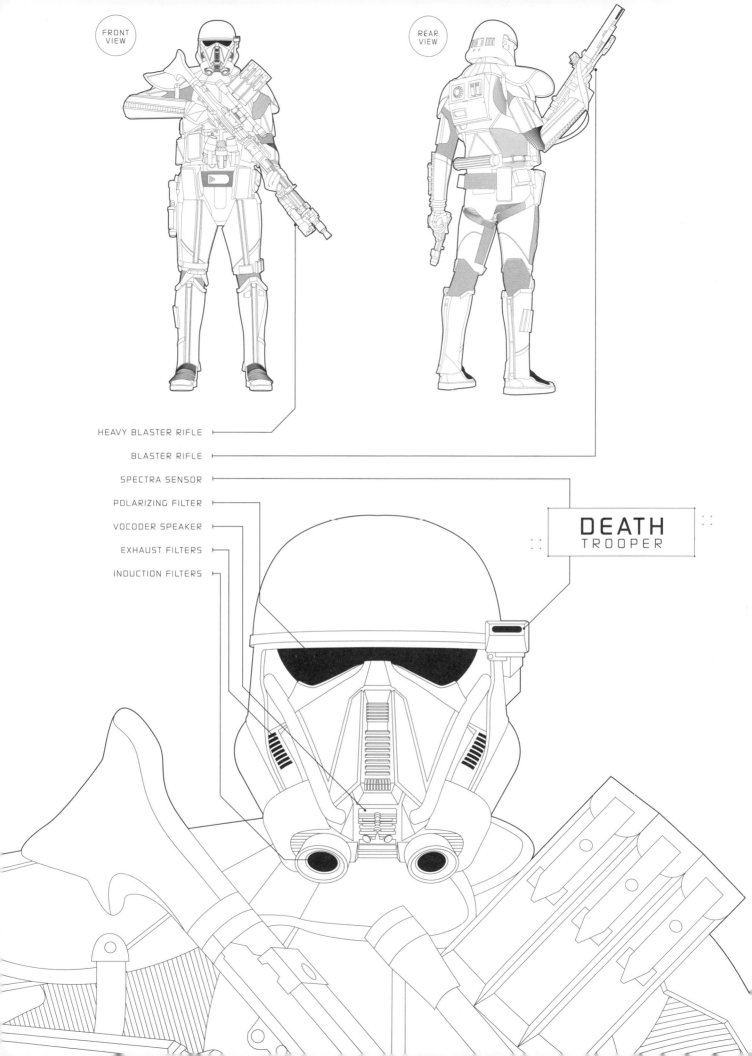

FRONT
VIEW

REAR
VIEW

HEAVY BLASTER RIFLE
BLASTER RIFLE
SPECTRA SENSOR
POLARIZING FILTER
VOCODER SPEAKER
EXHAUST FILTERS
INDUCTION FILTERS

DEATH
TROOPER

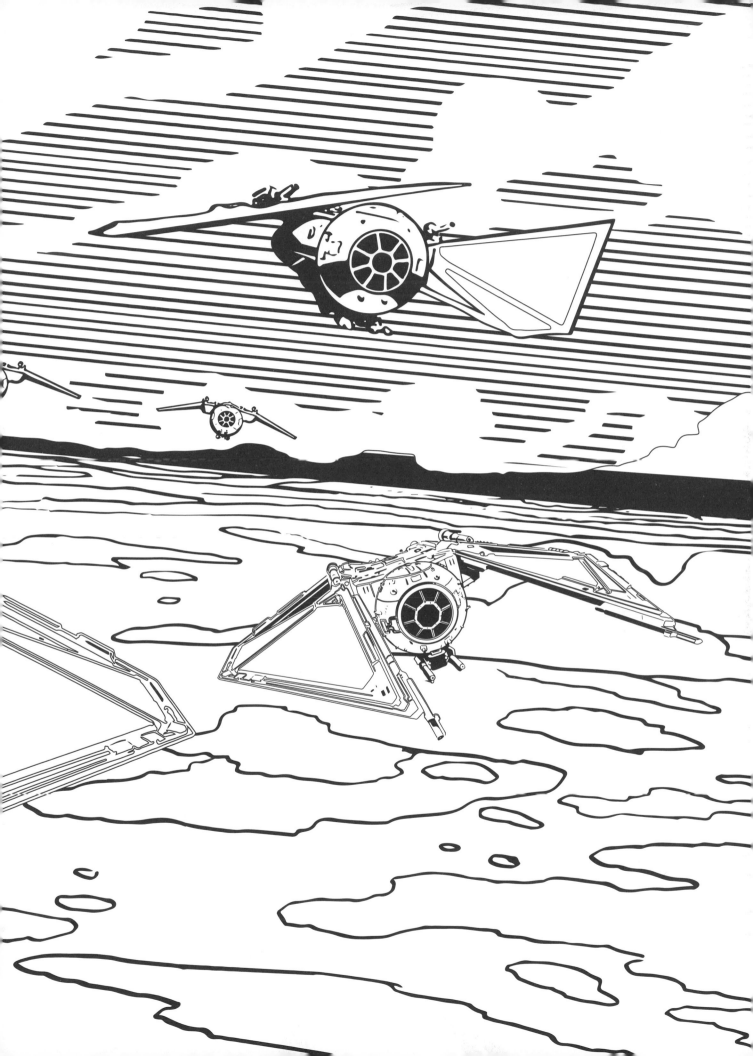

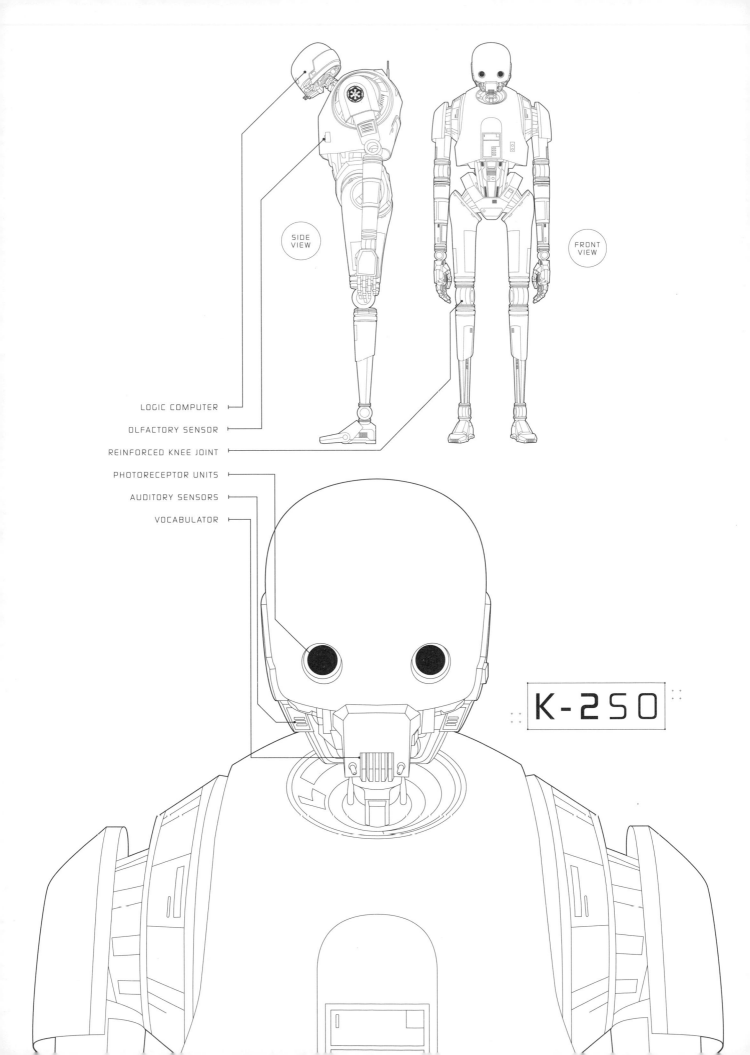

SIDE
VIEW

FRONT
VIEW

LOGIC COMPUTER ⊢

OLFACTORY SENSOR ⊢

REINFORCED KNEE JOINT ⊢

PHOTORECEPTOR UNITS ⊢

AUDITORY SENSORS ⊢

VOCABULATOR ⊢

K-2SO

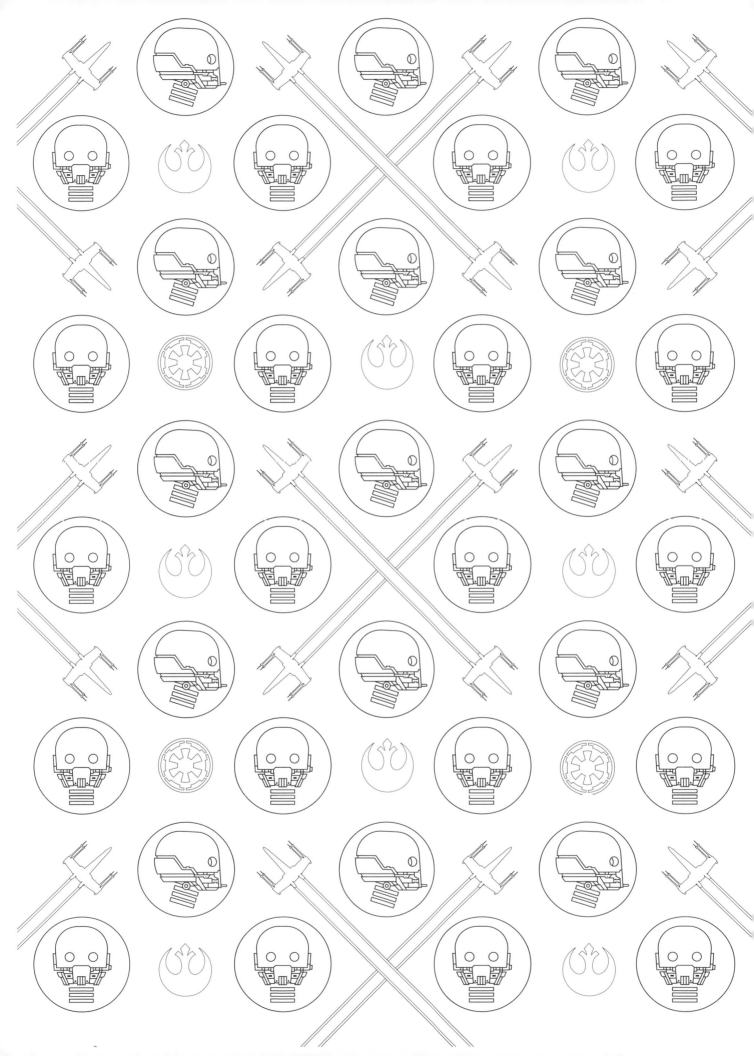

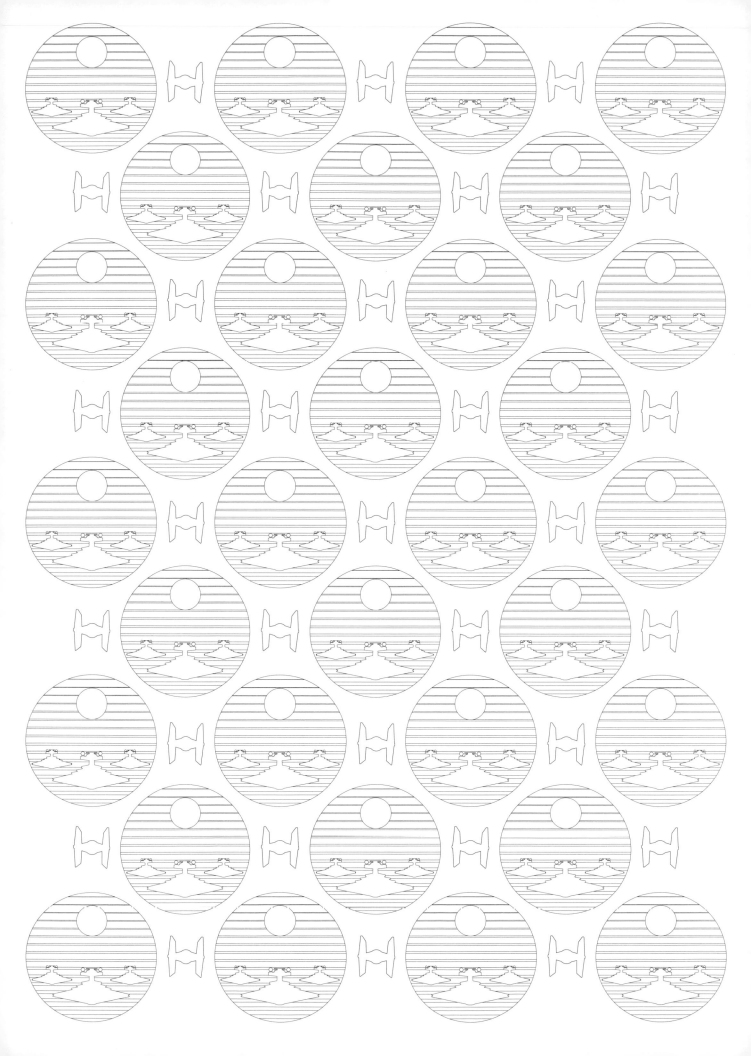

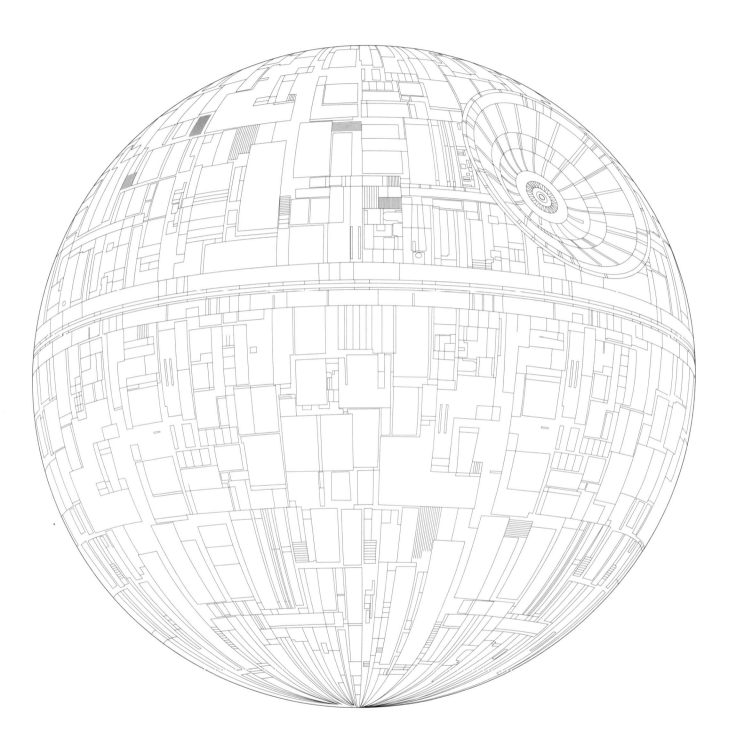

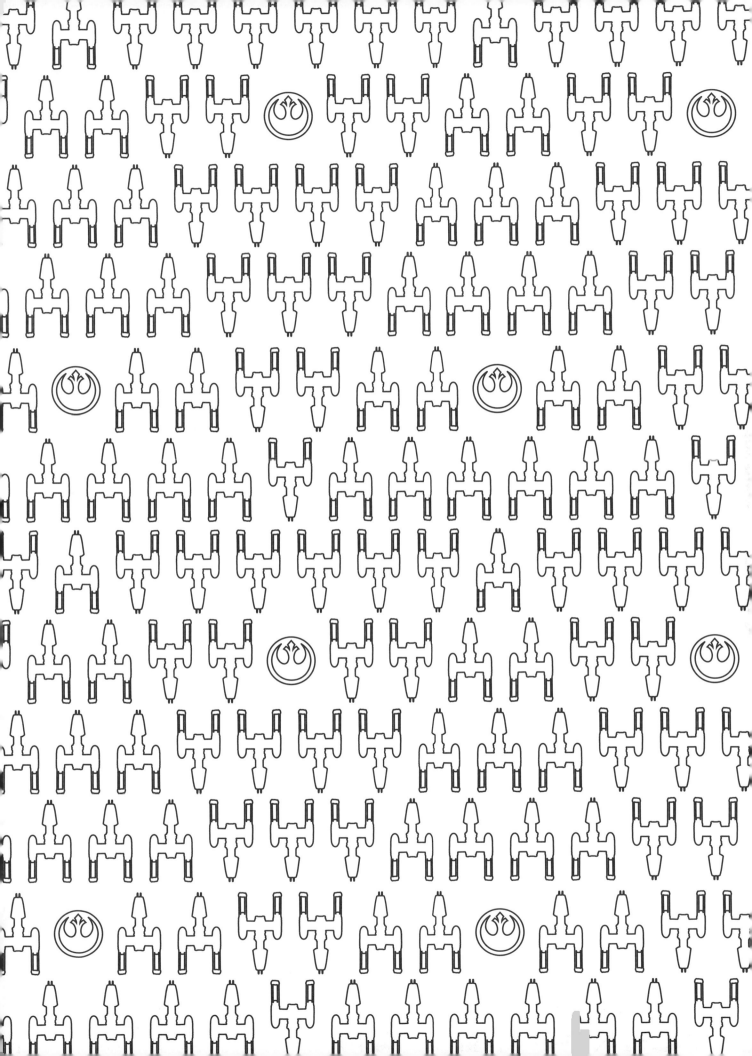

BAIL ORGANA

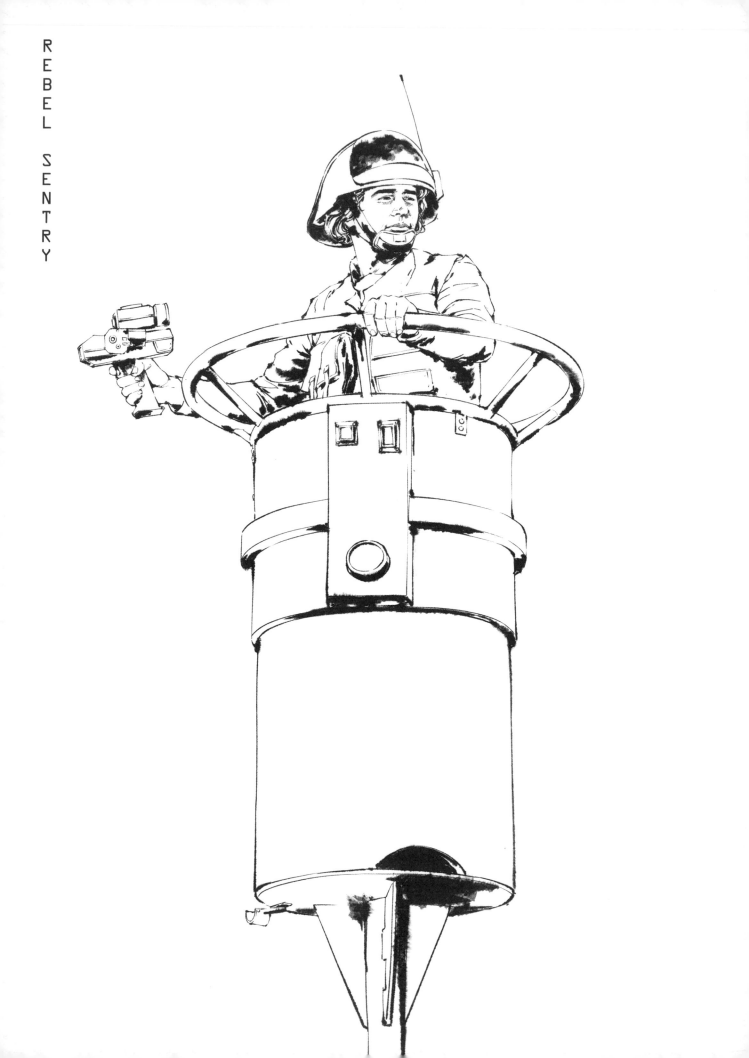

HOLY CITY PILGRIMS

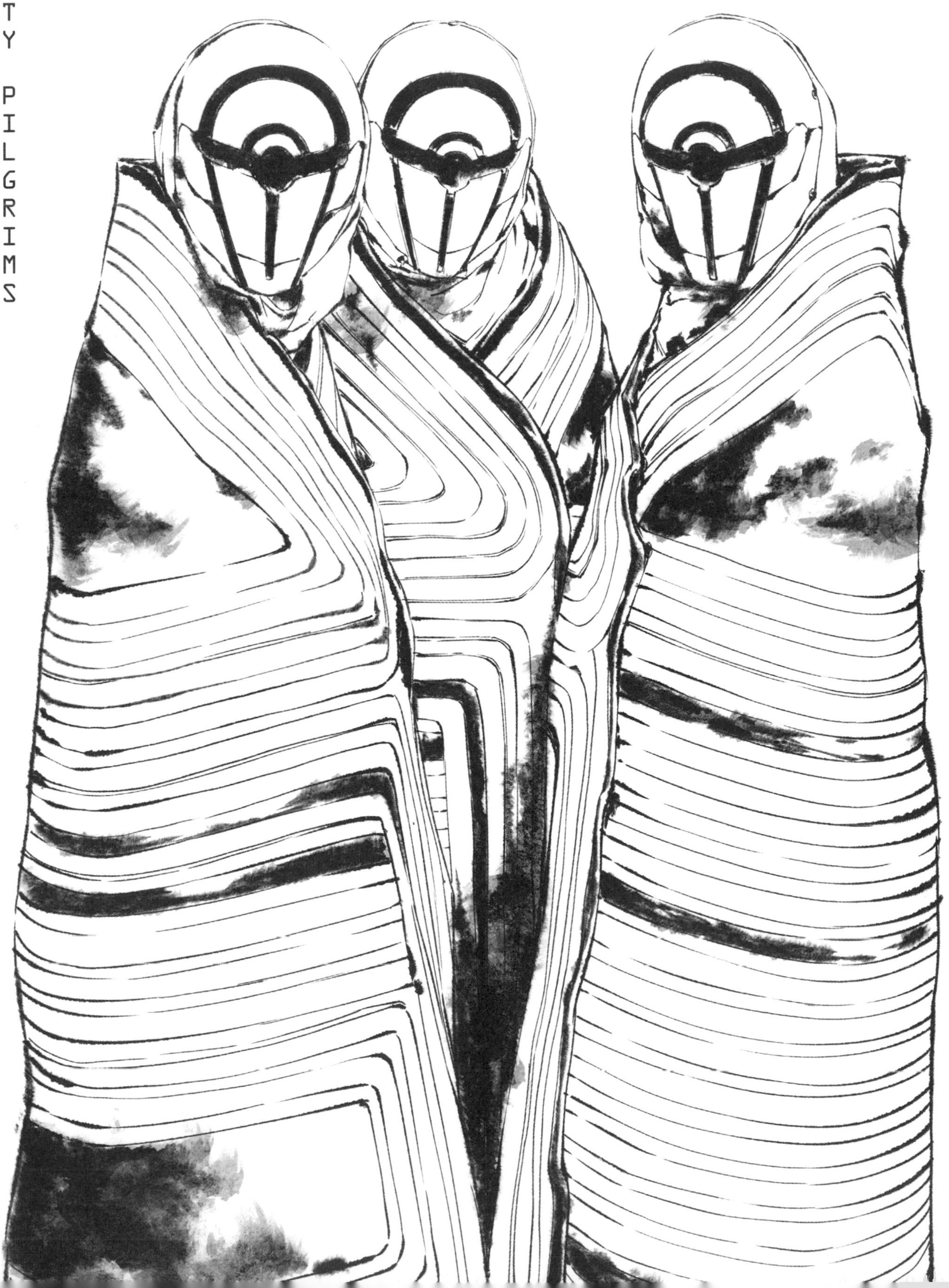

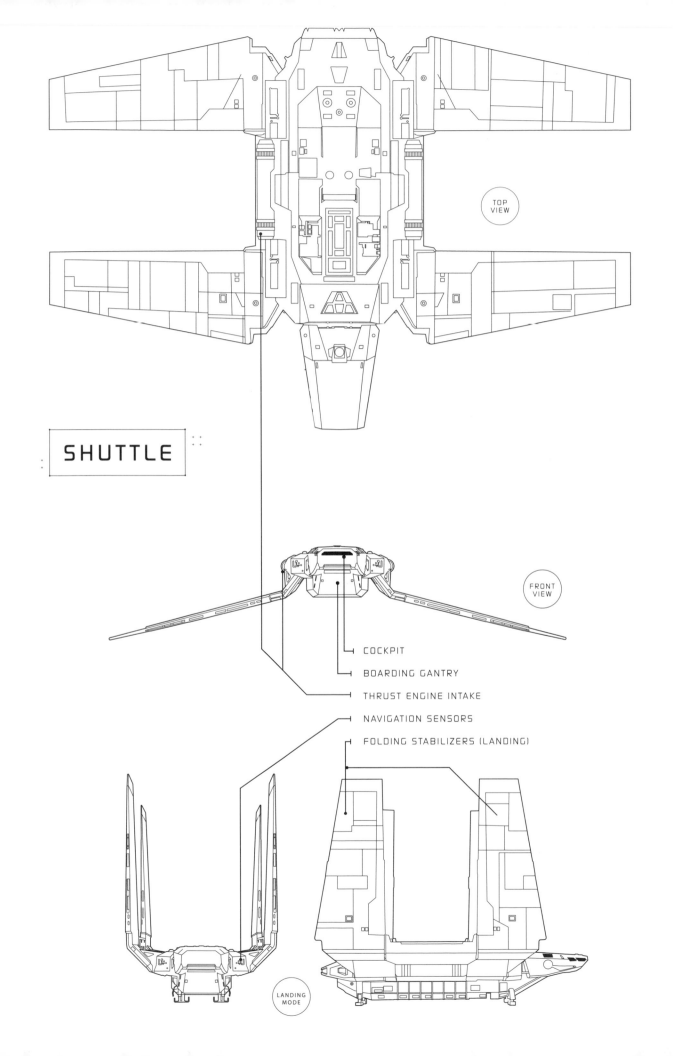

TOP
VIEW

SHUTTLE

FRONT
VIEW

COCKPIT

BOARDING GANTRY

THRUST ENGINE INTAKE

NAVIGATION SENSORS

FOLDING STABILIZERS (LANDING)

LANDING
MODE

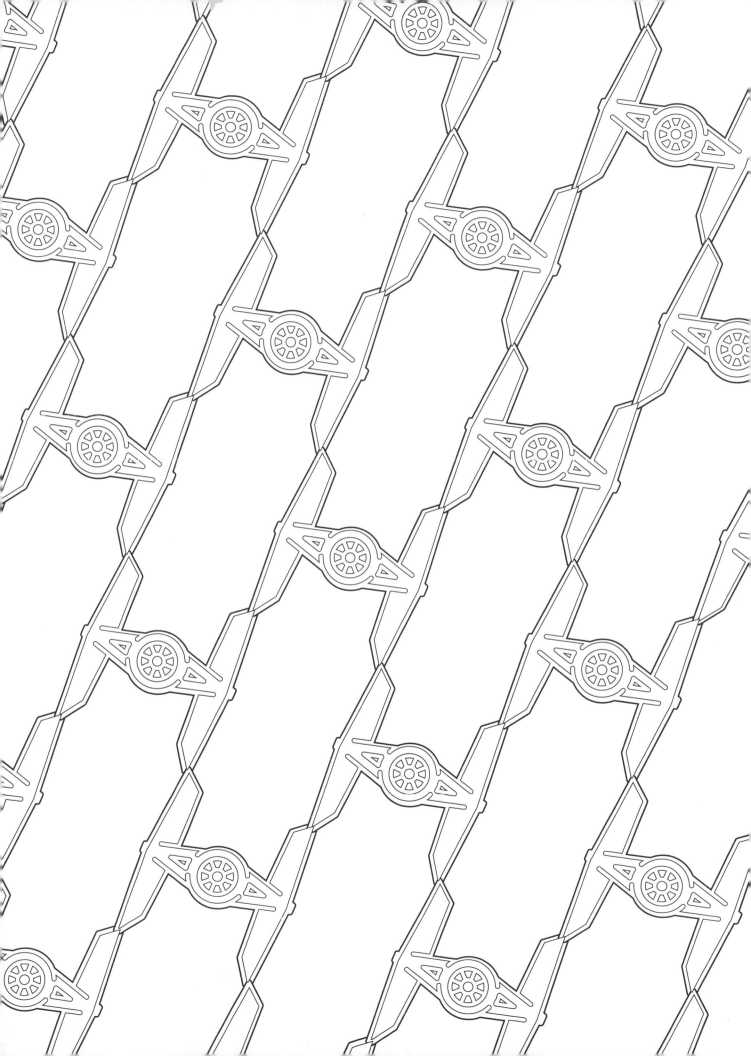

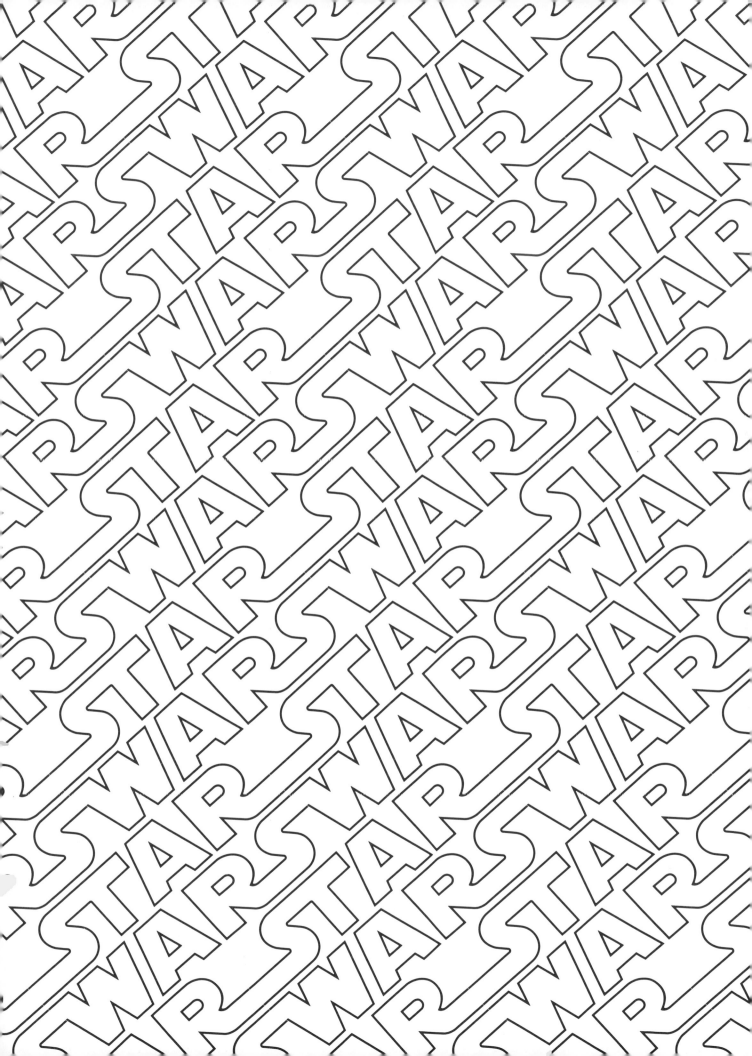

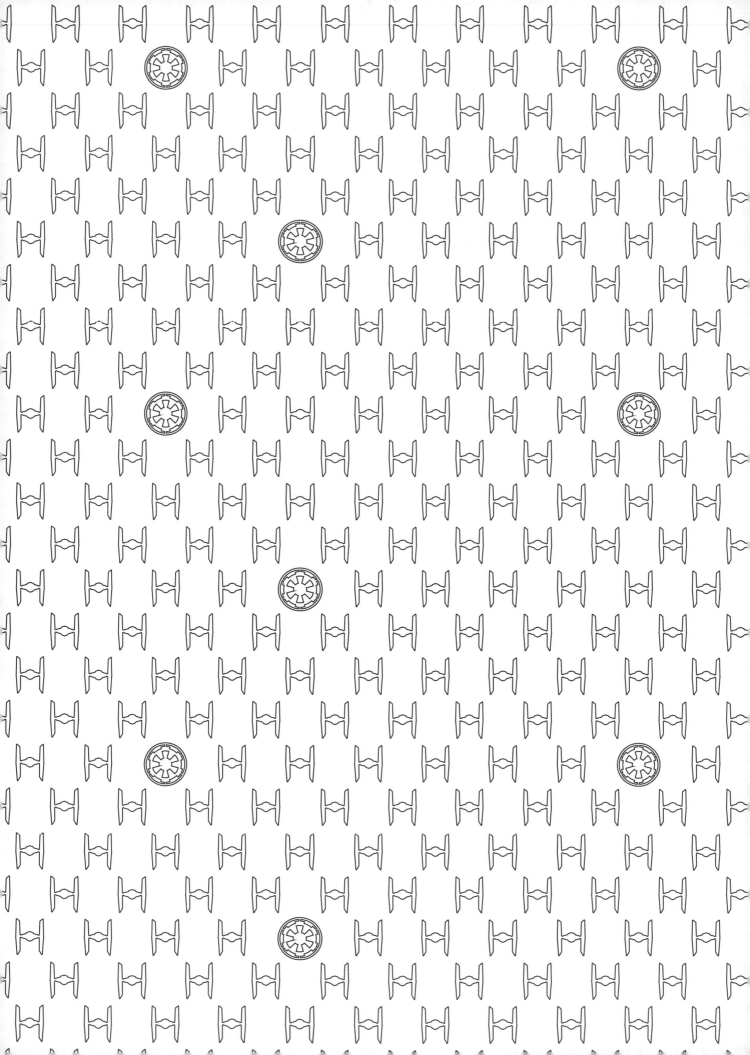

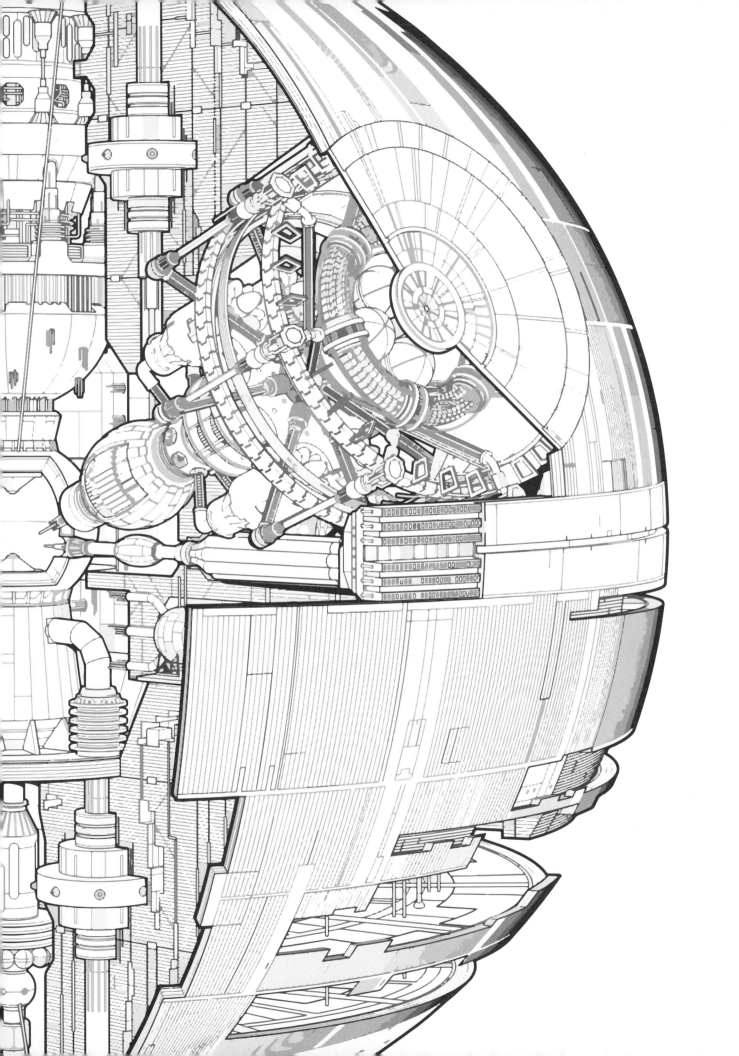

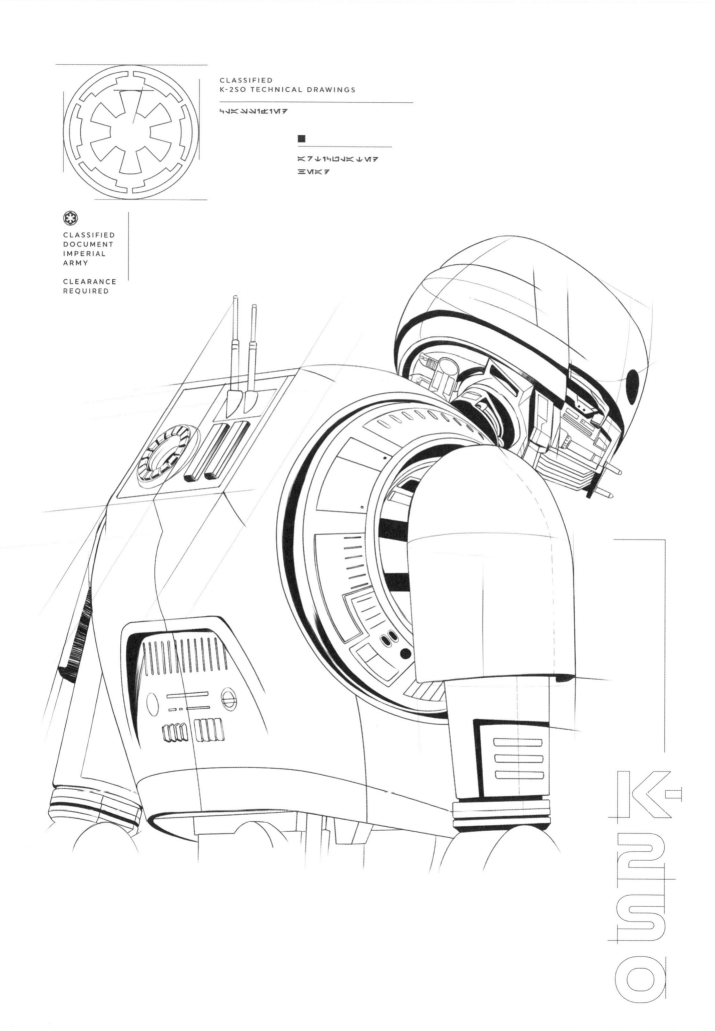

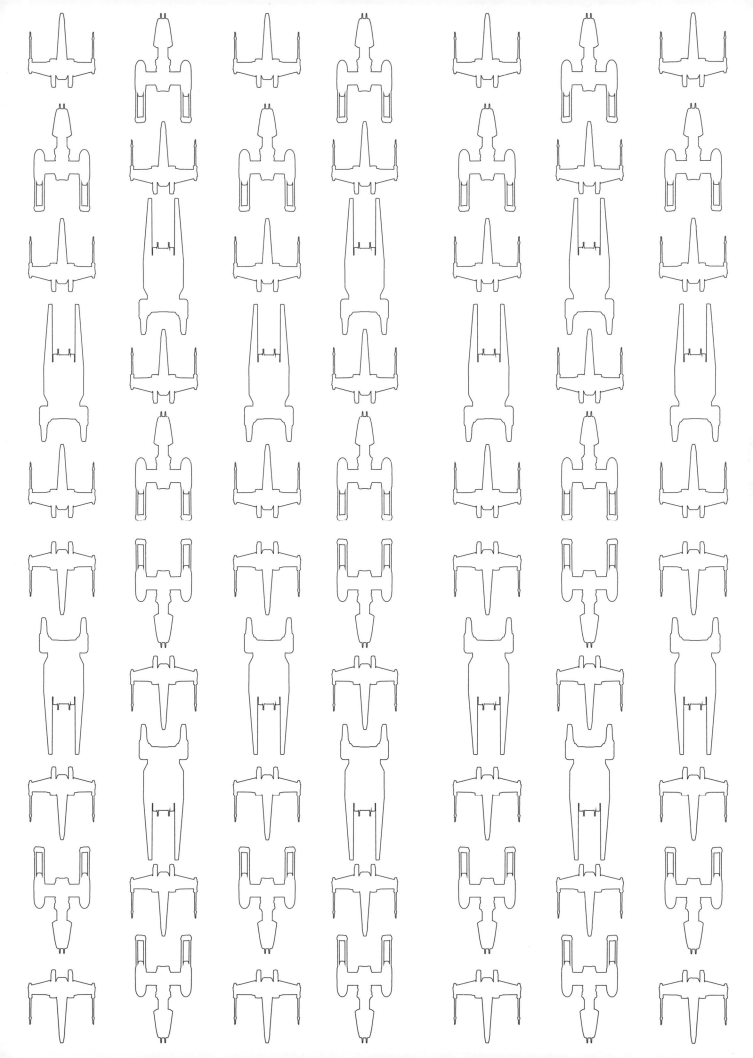

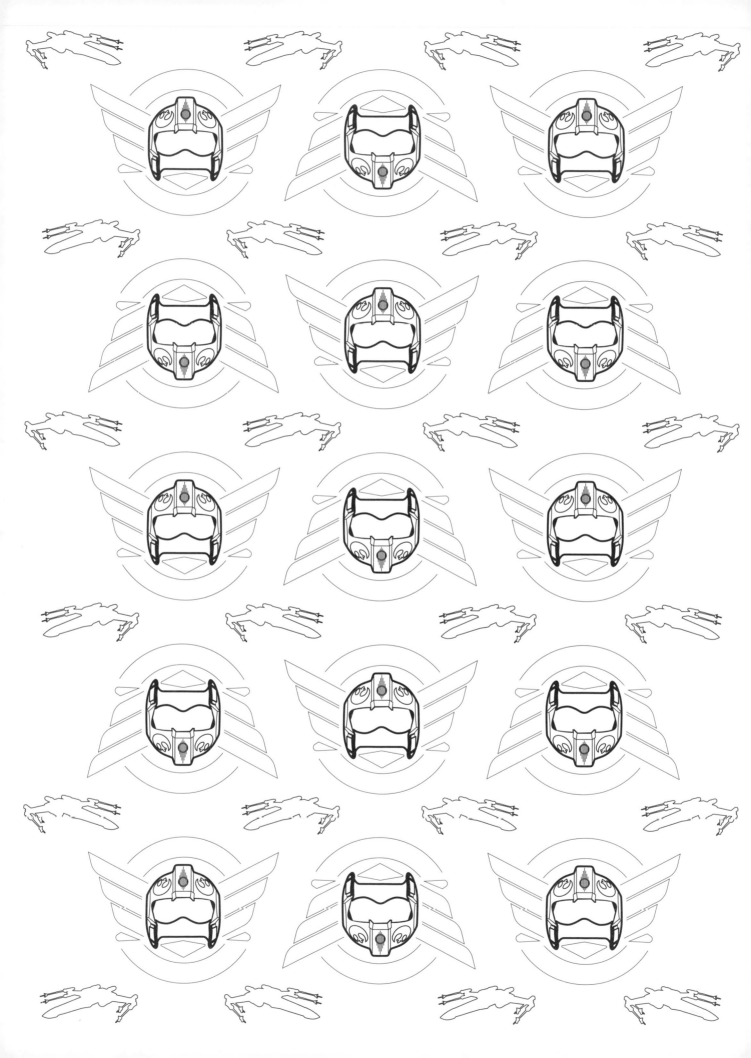

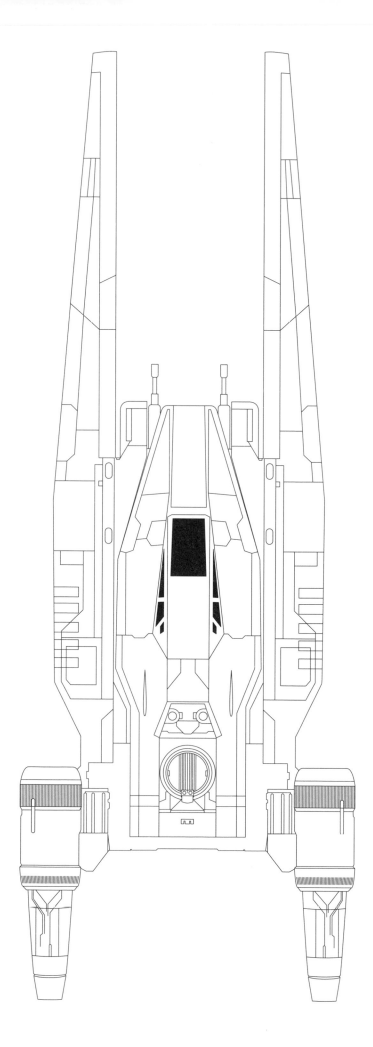

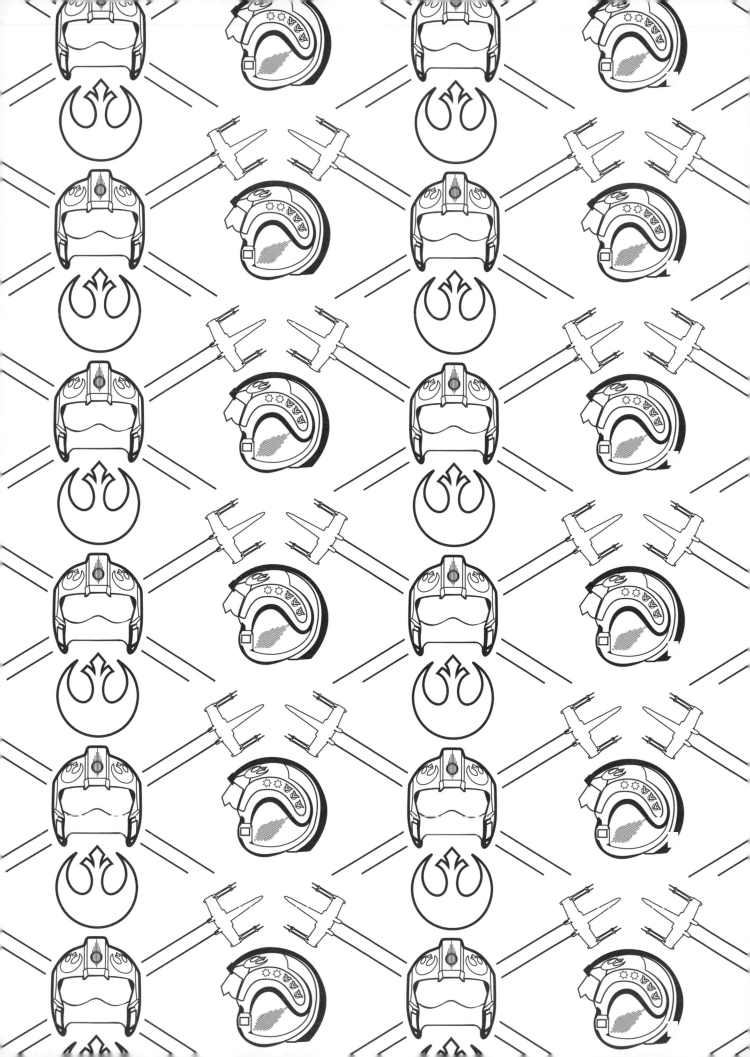

WEETEEF CYU-BEE

INNER
VIEW

SUPERLASER FOCUS LENS

SUPERLASER

COMMAND CENTER (NORTH)

POWER CELL COUPLING

REACTOR CORE

MAIN REACTOR

QUADANIUM STEEL HULL

EQUATORIAL TRENCH

DEATH STAR

OUTER
HULL

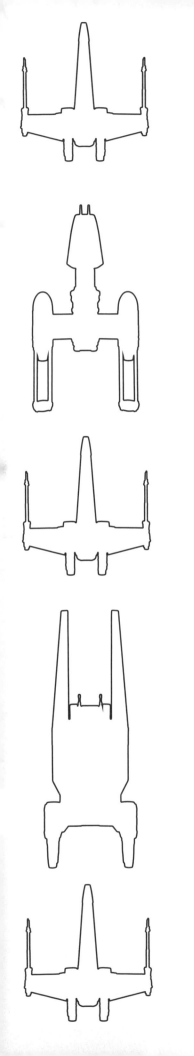
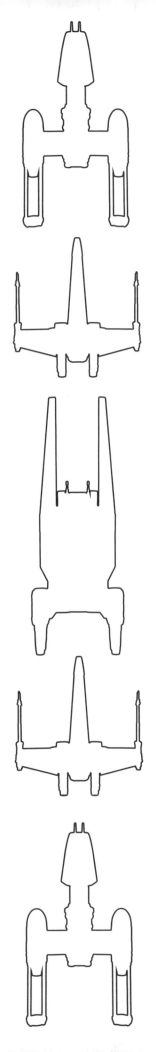
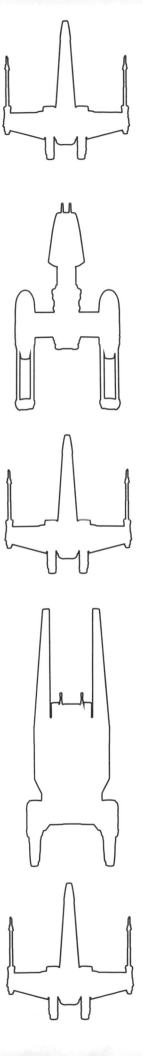
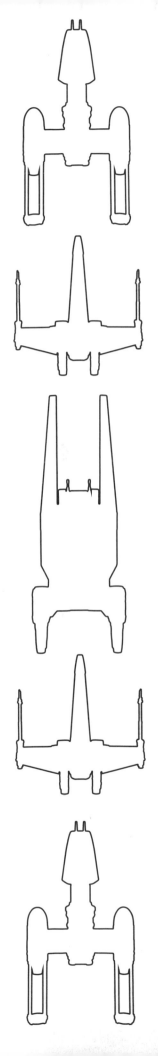

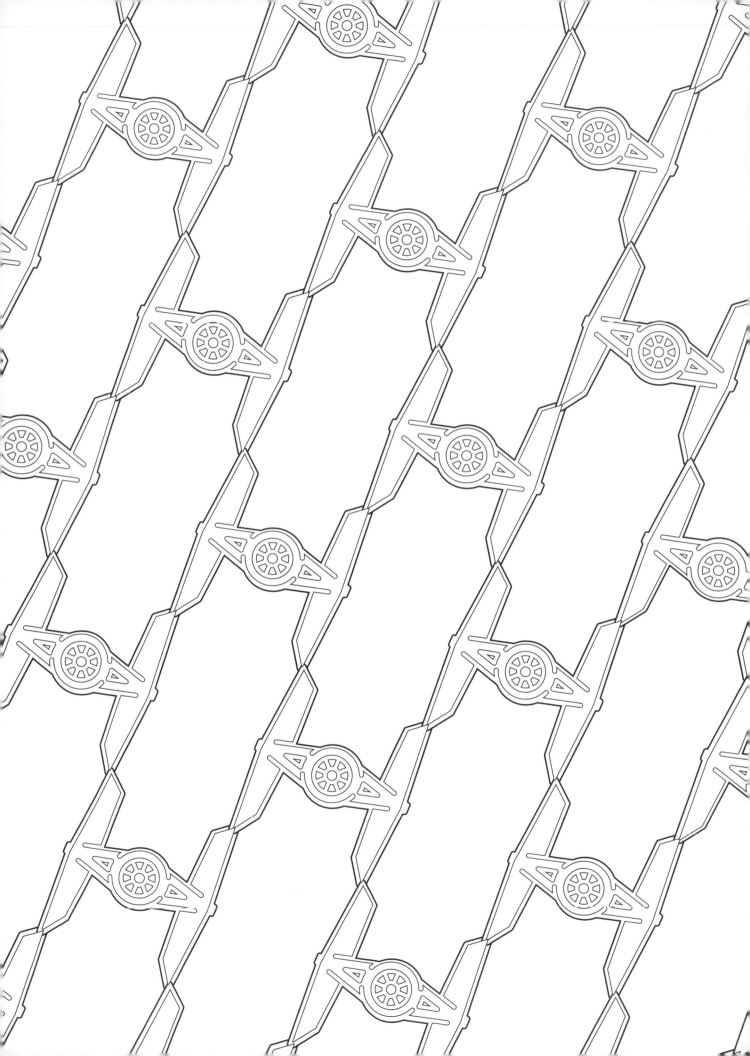

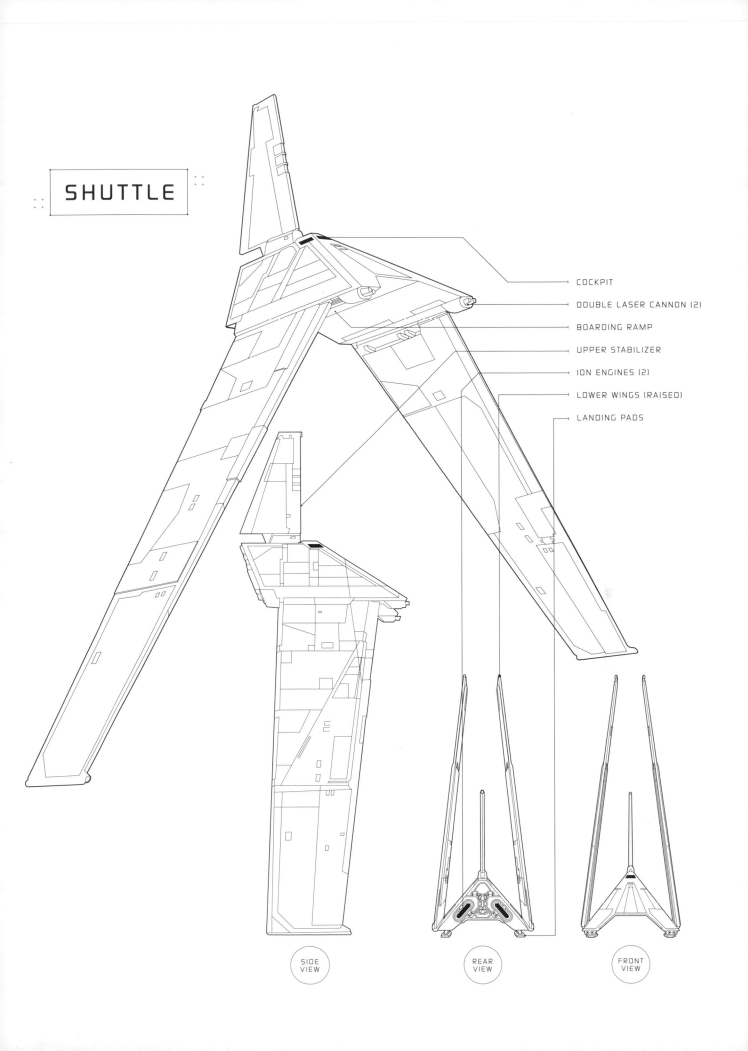

SHUTTLE

COCKPIT

DOUBLE LASER CANNON (2)

BOARDING RAMP

UPPER STABILIZER

ION ENGINES (2)

LOWER WINGS (RAISED)

LANDING PADS

SIDE
VIEW

REAR
VIEW

FRONT
VIEW

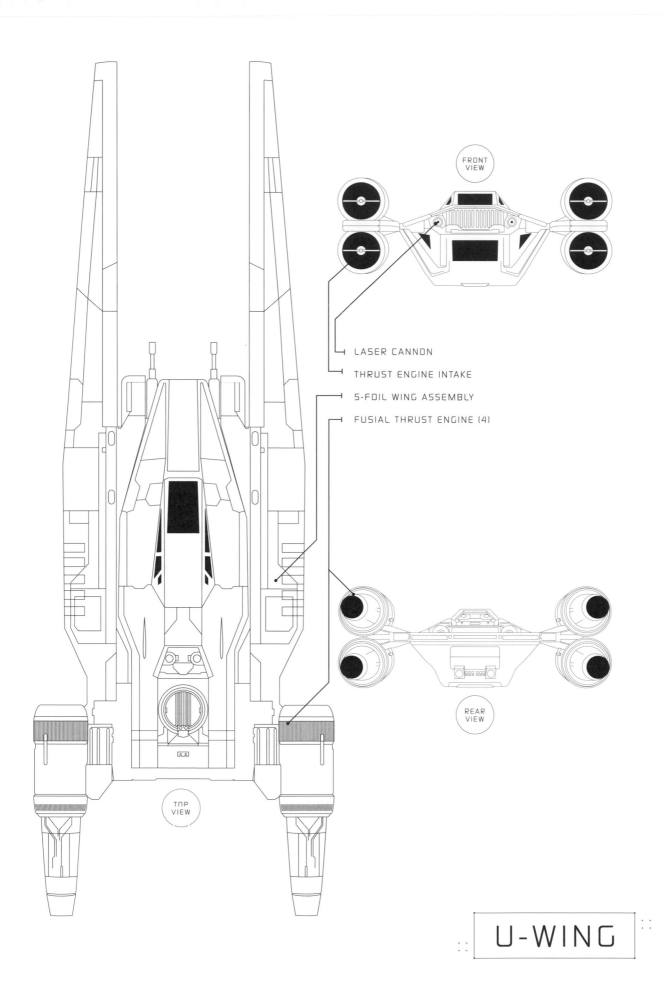

FRONT
VIEW

LASER CANNON

THRUST ENGINE INTAKE

S-FOIL WING ASSEMBLY

FUSIAL THRUST ENGINE (4)

REAR
VIEW

TOP
VIEW

U-WING

BISTAN

SCARIF TROOPER

IMPERIAL
SCARIF

DEFENCE
STATION

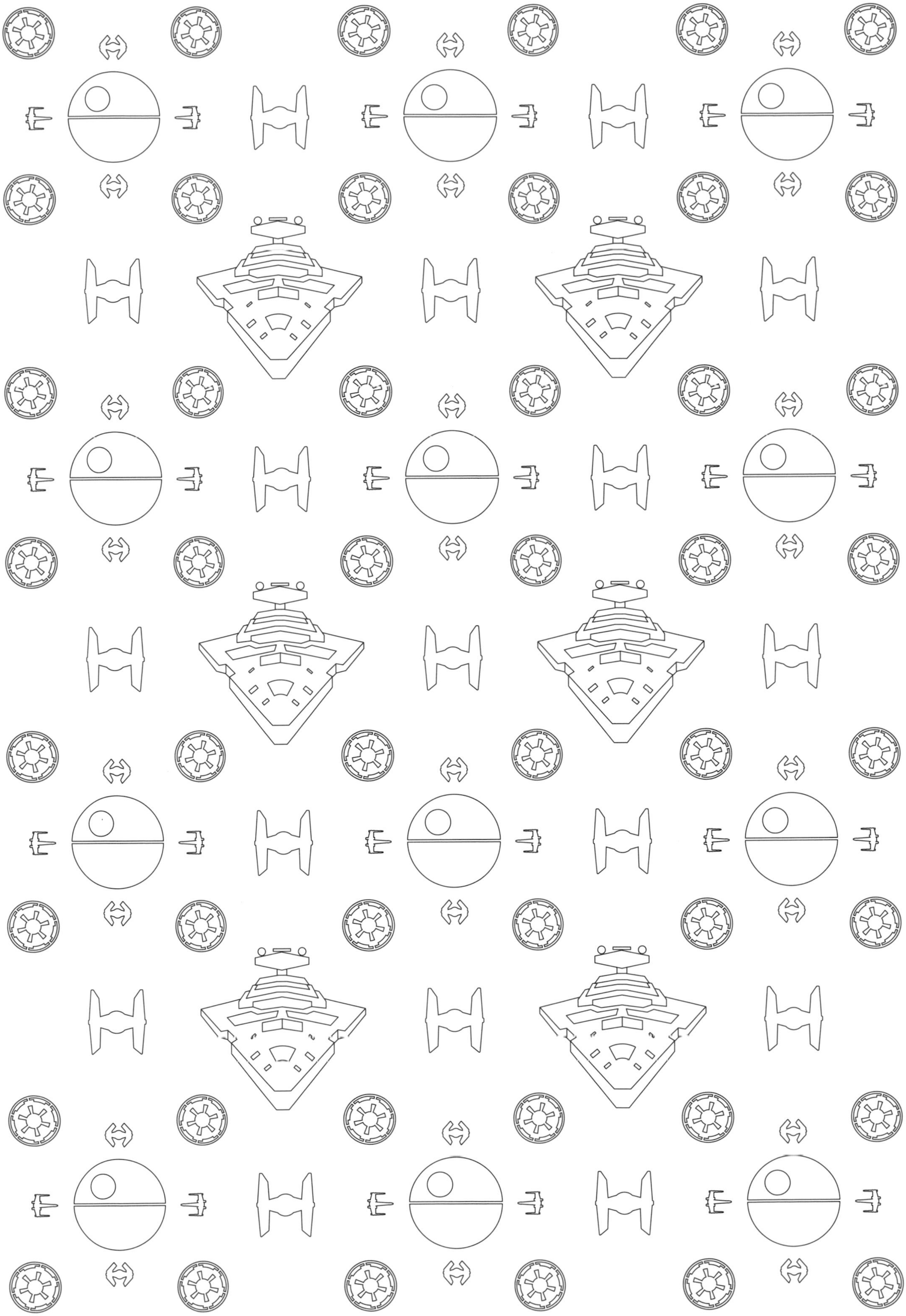

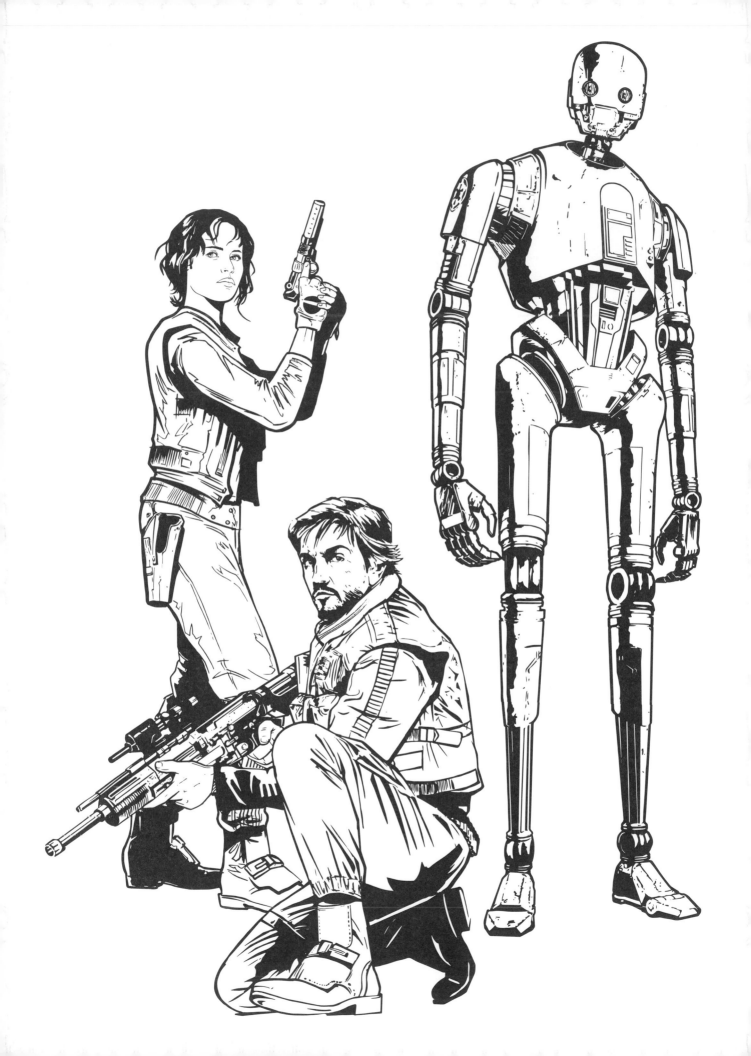

EGMONT

We bring stories to life

First published in Great Britain 2016
by Egmont UK Limited, The Yellow Building,
1 Nicholas Road, London W11 4AN

© & ™ 2016 Lucasfilm Ltd.

ISBN 978 1 4052 8637 4
67169/1
Printed in Italy

For more great *Star Wars* books, visit www.egmont.co.uk/starwars

Stay safe online. Any website addresses listed in this book are correct at the time of going to print.
However, Egmont is not responsible for content hosted by third parties. Please be aware that online
content can be subject to change and websites can contain content that is unsuitable for children.

We advise that all children are supervised when using the internet.